Free Association

Where My Mind Goes During Science Class

WRITTEN BY
BARBARA ESHAM

ILLUSTRATED BY
MIKE GORDON

Little
Pickle
Press

Click, click, click, click... Oh, right! I'm in **SCIENCE** class! The sound of Mrs. Freedman's shoes startled me back to class again.

Have you ever started to think about one thing and ended up thinking about something completely different? I do it all the time.

We're learning about the Arctic Circle in science. I was following along, but then I suddenly became distracted by one of my adventurous ideas.

I started thinking about my boogie board and how much fun it might be if I took it to the Arctic Circle.

"Emily, please pay attention. The test is next Monday, and I'm concerned you will not be prepared," Mrs. Freedman whispered as she turned four pages of my textbook.

I love science. Really, I do, but I can tell
Mrs. Freedman doesn't think so.

She has this extraordinary ability to catch me
right in the middle of what I'm **NOT** supposed to
be thinking about. I guess my daydream adventures
keep me from following along in class.

I have always loved exploring new ideas and doing experiments. I thought science was going to be my favorite class.

It seems like the only thing we do in science is memorize information from our book. Science class just doesn't feel like science to me. Is this what Albert Einstein did?

"Emily, I need you to pay attention.
You are two pages behind the class again,"
Mrs. Freedman said in her frustrated voice.

"I'm sorry, Mrs. Freedman. I was thinking about
Albert Einstein," I replied with a whisper.

"Well, Emily, I'm sure Albert Einstein would suggest that you follow along with the class," Mrs. Freedman added. The rest of the class giggled. I felt like crawling under my desk.

To make matters worse, Mrs. Freedman announced, "Emily Taylor, I would like to see you before lunch today."

I wish that I could just dig a hole to the other side of the world to escape this embarrassment.

My entire class went to lunch, but I stayed behind to talk with Mrs. Freedman.

She got right down to business.

"You are a smart girl, Emily, but I am concerned about the difficulty you are having with focusing in class," she said in a serious voice.

"I thought of an exercise that might help keep you on track.

The next time you daydream or become distracted during class, I would like for you to write about it in this journal," she said.

"Even if I'm thinking about riding a giant wave on my boogie board?"

"Yes, even if you are thinking about your boogie board," said Mrs. Freedman.

"The purpose of the exercise is to help you notice when you are distracted. I have a feeling this will help you recognize what is important, and what is **NOT** important to think about during science class," she added.

The next day in science class, I opened my
new journal, just in case I became distracted.

As we were learning more about the Arctic Circle,
I started thinking about some great ideas that
weren't exactly about what we were learning.

Mrs. Freedman might consider my ideas
distractions, so I began to write them
down in my journal, just in case.

Mrs. Freedman suddenly appeared behind me and whispered, "Emily, I would like to see you after class."

Oh no, I guess I'm in trouble again.

"Emily, you spent half the class writing!"
Mrs. Freedman exclaimed with a frown.

"Mrs. Freedman, I wrote all of my ideas in my journal. Some of my ideas are about science and the Arctic Circle, but not exactly what we were working on in class," I replied nervously.

"For a minute, I did daydream about my friend's sleepover this weekend and how we plan to polish her brother's nails while he is sleeping," I explained. I was blushing of course.

"I would like to read your journal to have a better understanding of what is distracting you in class," said Mrs. Freedman, as she gently took the journal from my hands.

Oh no! I wish that I hadn't mentioned the sleepover at all!
I only thought about it for a few seconds, and I stopped
daydreaming about it once I wrote in the journal.

How will I ever become a scientist if I can't make it
through fourth grade science?

The next day Mrs. Freedman seemed very happy. She was holding my journal and smiling.

"Class, one of your classmates has created a theory to explore the differences between penguins and flight birds. She has also made a list of changes she believes penguins would need in order to survive in a warmer environment."

"From now on, each of you can create a science journal to let your inventive imaginations soar! This is what science is all about—creating new ideas and using your imaginations," Mrs. Freedman said with a smile.

During lunch, Mrs. Freedman came up to me and said, "Emily, your creative thinking skills are quite advanced for a student your age."

"Thank you, Mrs. Freedman...but what
creative thinking skills are we talking about?"
I asked with a nervous laugh.

"Your penguin theory, of course. Remember this, Emily Taylor: theories, creative thought, and persistence, along with a bit of tolerance for the required work, will lead you to success."

"Oh! **THOSE** creative thinking skills! I was afraid
you were going to mention my theory on the best
way to polish Claire's brother's fingernails."

Mrs. Freedman giggled, "I am sure your theory will help you discover the best way to complete that experiment."

Are YOU an EVERYDAY GENIUS too?

Everyday geniuses are **creative,** STRONG, **thoughtful,**
and sometimes learn a little differently from others.
And that's what makes them so special!

In *Free Association*, Emily has a hard time focusing in class. Her mind wanders and she loses her place in her textbook.

Have you ever daydreamed when you were supposed to pay attention?

What happened?

Mrs. Freedman gives Emily a journal to write down all the thoughts she has when her mind wanders during science class. That's just one way you can help your mind deal with extra thoughts.

Here are a few other things you can do:
- Breathe. When you notice your mind starting to wander, take a deep breath. Focusing on your breathing can help bring you back to focus.
- Rest. Sometimes a restless mind is the result of a tired body. Make sure you're getting plenty of restful sleep at night.
- Move. Getting enough exercise and eating healthy foods also make a difference in the way your mind functions.

What are some other ways you can help stay focused?

Your mind is a wonderful and powerful part of your body. And even the smartest scientists have not figured out all that our brains are capable of. So don't feel like you have to do this all on your own! Ask a caring adult for help—a parent, teacher, librarian, aunt, cousin, coach—anyone who can help you find the resources you need.

Remember, everyday geniuses are creative, strong, thoughtful, and sometimes learn a little differently from others. It's never a bad thing to be different—embracing and learning from our differences is what makes the world a better place!

"**This is a wonderful book series**. Each story shows children that success is about effort and determination, that problems need not derail them, and that adults can understand their worries and struggles. My research demonstrates that these lessons are essential for children."

—Dr. Carol S. Dweck, Stanford University professor of psychology

Carol Dweck is the author of Mindset: The New Psychology of Success. *Her scholarly book* Self-Theories: Their Role in Motivation, Personality, and Development *was named Book of the Year by the World Education Fellowship. Dr. Dweck is one of the world's leading researchers in the field of motivation and is the Virginia Eaton Professor of Psychology at Stanford University.*

· · · · · ●

"**Today's children are taught to pay attention** at all times, follow rules unquestioningly, and do well on one-size-fits-all tests. Mountains of psychological research clearly show how none of this is conducive to creativity and innovation. In the Adventures of Everyday Geniuses series, Esham knows her cognitive psychology and the best ways to learn and create. She brilliantly presents entertaining, relatable stories while highlighting the importance of individual differences and the use of imagination and daydreaming. I really wish I read these books when I was younger, I know I would have felt a lot better about myself!"

—Scott Barry Kaufman, PhD, New York University professor of psychology, Department of Psychology

"**The Adventures of Everyday Geniuses** is simply an outstanding series of books. By sharing stories about kids who learn in a variety of ways, Barbara Esham helps students who identify with these characters to become more self-confident, and to better understand how they learn. These books are also of great benefit for parents and classmates, because they portray differences among learners in a positive light. They also highlight the importance of environment and parental and teacher support in the cultivation of critical thinkers and lovers of learning. As an experienced educator, I can confidently say that these books should be a staple in every elementary classroom."

—Dr. Corinne Hyde, University of Southern California associate (teaching) professor of clinical education, Ed.D.

· · · · · ●

"**As an affective neuroscientist and an educational psychologist**, I can tell you that two things are especially important for children's school learning: feeling emotionally validated and having a good awareness of one's own learning. These books offer a rare combination for young students—they teach both of these things!"

—Dr. Mary Helen Immordino-Yang, University of Southern California professor of psychology at the Brain and Creativity Institute, Neuroscience Graduate Program Faculty

FOR MORE ENDORSEMENTS, REVIEWS, RESOURCES, AND EVEN LESSON PLANS, PLEASE VISIT JABBERWOCKYKIDS.COM

About the Author

Author Barbara Esham was one of those kids who couldn't resist performing a pressure test on a pudding cup. She has always been a "free association" thinker, finding life far more interesting while in a state of abstract thought. Barbara lives on the East Coast with her three daughters. Together, in Piagetian fashion, they have explored the ideas and theories behind the definitions of intelligence, creativity, learning, and success. Barb researches and writes from her home office, in the spare time available between car pools, homework, and bedtime.

About the Illustrator

Cartooning has brought Mike Gordon acclaim in worldwide competitions, adding to his international reputation as a top humorous illustrator. Since 1993 he has continued his successful career based in California, gaining a nomination in the prestigious National Cartoonist Society Awards. Mike is the renowned illustrator for the wildly popular book series beginning with *Do Princesses Wear Hiking Boots?*

Copyright © 2013 by Barbara Esham
Cover and internal design © 2018 by Sourcebooks, Inc.
Text by Barbara Esham
Illustrations by Mike Gordon
Digital color by Molly Hahn

Sourcebooks and the colophon are registered trademarks of Sourcebooks, Inc.

The characters and events portrayed in this book are fictitious and are used fictitiously. Any similarity to real persons, living or dead, is purely coincidental and not intended by the author.

The story text was set in OpenDyslexic, a font specifically designed for readability with dyslexia.
The back matter was set in Adobe Garamond Pro.

All rights reserved.

Published by Little Pickle Press, an imprint of Sourcebooks Jabberwocky
P.O. Box 4410, Naperville, Illinois 60567-4410
(630) 961-3900
Fax: (630) 961-2168
sourcebooks.com

Source of Production: Leo Paper, Heshan City, Guangdong Province, China
Date of Production: February 2018
Run Number: 5011331

Printed and bound in China.
LEO 10 9 8 7 6 5 4 3 2 1

THE
ADVENTURES
⁙F EVERYDAY
GENIUSES